The Unconditional Love Part 1

Kavita Thomas

pencil

ISBN **978-93-5667-150-8**
© Kavita Thomas 2022
Published in India 2022 by Pencil

A brand of
One Point Six Technologies Pvt. Ltd.
123, Building J2, Shram Seva Premises,
Wadala Truck Terminal, Wadala (E)
Mumbai 400037, Maharashtra, INDIA
E connect@thepencilapp.com
W www.thepencilapp.com

DISCLAIMER: *This is a work of fiction. Names, characters, places, events and incidents are the products of the author's imagination. The opinions expressed in this book do not seek to reflect the views of the Publisher.*

Author biography

This is first time writer Kavita Thomas.Hope the readers like this first official effort.

This work is purely fictional and does not have any resemblance to anyone's life whatsoever.

CONTENTS

Repeat 2

This is first time writer Kavita Thomas.Hope the readers like this first official effort.

This work is purely fictional and does not have any resemblance to anyone's life whatsoever.

Chapter 1

Neil Roy is a well-known actor and superstar in India. His secretary Mr Tandon comes to meet him on a regular Monday morning. 'Good morning Neil , how are you this morning.? Neil replies 'Very well Mr Tandon .'Mr Tandon then enquires about the party Neil attended 'How was the party last night Neil?' Neil replies with a smile it was okay you know I dont much like attending such parties much. ' Mr Tandon says 'Well Neil you know as a superstar you are expected to attend such parties. ' Neil says to Mr Tandon 'Yes and I'm counting on you for all this. Mr Tandon happily 'Certainly Sir Neil then asks about his schedule 'So Mr Tandon what is my schedule for today for today?' Mr Tandon goes on 'Sir you have the shoot at 11 pm for Reena's movie , thereafter they are also having a nice time a get together for lunch on the set for the success of the film's first look. Neil 'Oh that should be fine what next?' Mr Tandon goes on 'Thereafter you have a shoot for Entertainment production company 'Oh Mr Tandon please shift that film shoot further for a while .I'mnptenjoyi g this particular shoot and I feel we should shift this film further and start working more on Sheena's father's film . This film is going very well and I'm having a very positive feeling of this film. Mr Tandon 'As you wish Neil, the work does look promising. '
is first time writer Kavita Thomas.Hope the readers like

first official effort.Neil Roy is a well-known actor and superstar in India. His secretary Mr Tandon comes to meet him on a regular Monday morning. 'Good morning Neil , how are you this morning.? Neil replies 'Very well Mr Tandon .'Mr Tandon then enquires about the party Neil attended 'How was the party last night Neil?' Neil replies with a smile it was okay you know I dont much like attending such parties much. ' Mr Tandon says 'Well Neil you know as a superstar you are expected to attend such parties. ' Neil says to Mr Tandon 'Yes and I'm counting on you for all this. Mr Tandon happily 'Certainly Sir Neil then asks about his schedule 'So Mr Tandon what is my schedule for today for today?' Mr Tandon goes on 'Sir you have the shoot at 11 pm for Reena's movie , thereafter they are also having a nice time a get together for lunch on the set for the success of the film's first look. Neil 'Oh that should be fine what next?' Mr Tandon goes on 'Thereafter you have a shoot for Entertainment production company 'Oh Mr Tandon please shift that film shoot further for a while .I'mnptenjoyi g this particular shoot and I feel we should shift this film further and start working more on Sheena's father's film . This film is going very well and I'm having a very positive feeling of this film. Mr Tandon 'As you wish Neil, the work does look promising. '

Neil Roy is a well-known actor and superstar in India. His secretary Mr Tandon comes to meet him on a regular Monday morning. 'Good morning Neil , how are you this morning.? Neil replies 'Very well Mr Tandon .'Mr Tandon then enquires about the party

Neil attended 'How was the party last night Neil?' Neil replies with a smile it was okay you know I dont much like attending such parties much. ' Mr Tandon says 'Well Neil you know as a superstar you are expected to attend such parties. ' Neil says to Mr Tandon 'Yes and I'm counting on you for all this. Mr Tandon happily 'Certainly Sir Neil then asks about his schedule 'So Mr Tandon what is my schedule for today for today?' Mr Tandon goes on 'Sir you have the shoot at 11 pm for Reena's movie , thereafter they are also having a nice time a get together for lunch on the set for the success of the film's first look. Neil 'Oh that should be fine what next?' Mr Tandon goes on 'Thereafter you have a shoot for Entertainment production company 'Oh Mr Tandon please shift that film shoot further for a while .I'mnptenjoyi g this particular shoot and I feel we should shift this film further and start working more on Sheena's father's film . This film is going very well and I'm having a very positive feeling of this film. Mr Tandon 'As you wish Neil, the work does look promising. '

Neil Roy is a well-known actor and superstar in India. His secretary Mr Tandon comes to meet him on a regular Monday morning. 'Good morning Neil , how are you this morning.? Neil replies 'Very well Mr Tandon .'Mr Tandon then enquires about the party Neil attended 'How was the party last night Neil?' Neil replies with a smile it was okay you know I dont much like attending such parties much. ' Mr Tandon says 'Well Neil you know as a superstar you are expected to attend such parties. ' Neil says to Mr

Tandon 'Yes and I'm counting on you for all this. Mr Tandon happily 'Certainly Sir Neil then asks about his schedule 'So Mr Tandon what is my schedule for today for today?' Mr Tandon goes on 'Sir you have the shoot at 11 pm for Reena's movie , thereafter they are also having a nice time a get together for lunch on the set for the success of the film's first look. Neil 'Oh that should be fine what next?' Mr Tandon goes on 'Thereafter you have a shoot for Entertainment production company 'Oh Mr Tandon please shift that film shoot further for a while .I'mnptenjoyi g this particular shoot and I feel we should shift this film further and start working more on Sheena's father's film . This film is going very well and I'm having a very positive feeling of this film. Mr Tandon 'As you wish Neil, the work does look promising. '

Neil Roy is a well-known actor and superstar in India. His secretary Mr Tandon comes to meet him on a regular Monday morning. 'Good morning Neil , how are you this morning.? Neil replies 'Very well Mr Tandon .'Mr Tandon then enquires about the party Neil attended 'How was the party last night Neil?' Neil replies with a smile it was okay you know I dont much like attending such parties much. ' Mr Tandon says 'Well Neil you know as a superstar you are expected to attend such parties. ' Neil says to Mr Tandon 'Yes and I'm counting on you for all this. Mr Tandon happily 'Certainly Sir Neil then asks about his schedule 'So Mr Tandon what is my schedule for today for today?' Mr Tandon goes on 'Sir you have the shoot at 11 pm for Reena's movie , thereafter they are also having a nice time a get together for lunch on the set for the success of the film's first look. Neil 'Oh that should be fine what next?' Mr Tandon goes on 'Thereafter you have a shoot for Entertainment production company 'Oh Mr Tandon please shift that film shoot further for a while .I'mnptenjoyi g this particular shoot and I feel we should shift this film further and start working more on Sheena's father's film . This film is going very well and I'm having a very positive feeling of this film. Mr Tandon 'As you wish Neil, the work does look promising. '

Neil Roy is a well-known actor and superstar in India. His secretary Mr Tandon comes to meet him on a regular Monday morning. 'Good morning Neil , how are you this morning.? Neil replies 'Very well Mr Tandon .'Mr Tandon then enquires about the party Neil attended 'How was the party last night Neil?' Neil replies with a smile it was okay you know I dont much like attending such parties much. ' Mr Tandon says 'Well Neil you know as a superstar you are expected to attend such parties. ' Neil says to Mr Tandon 'Yes and I'm counting on you for all this. Mr Tandon happily 'Certainly Sir Neil then asks about his schedule 'So Mr Tandon what is my schedule for today for today?' Mr Tandon goes on 'Sir you have the shoot at 11 pm for Reena's movie , thereafter they are also having a nice time a get together for lunch on the set for the success of the film's first look. Neil 'Oh that should be fine what next?' Mr Tandon goes on 'Thereafter you have a shoot for Entertainment production company 'Oh Mr

Tandon please shift that film shoot further for a while .I'mnptenjoyi g this particular shoot and I feel we should shift this film further and start working more on Sheena's father's film . This film is going very well and I'm having a very positive feeling of this film. Mr Tandon 'As you wish Neil, the work does look promising. '

Neil Roy is a well-known actor and superstar in India. His secretary Mr Tandon comes to meet him on a regular Monday morning. 'Good morning Neil , how are you this morning.? Neil replies 'Very well Mr Tandon .'Mr Tandon then enquires about the party Neil attended 'How was the party last night Neil?' Neil replies with a smile it was okay you know I dont much like attending such parties much. ' Mr Tandon says 'Well Neil you know as a superstar you are expected to attend such parties. ' Neil says to Mr Tandon 'Yes and I'm counting on you for all this. Mr Tandon happily 'Certainly Sir Neil then asks about his schedule 'So Mr Tandon what is my schedule for today for today?' Mr Tandon goes on 'Sir you have the shoot at 11 pm for Reena's movie , thereafter they are also having a nice time a get together for lunch on the set for the success of the film's first look. Neil 'Oh that should be fine what next?' Mr Tandon goes on 'Thereafter you have a shoot for Entertainment production company 'Oh Mr Tandon please shift that film shoot further for a while .I'mnptenjoyi g this particular shoot and I feel we should shift this film further and start working more on Sheena's father's film . This film is going very well and I'm having a very positive feeling of this film. Mr Tandon 'As you wish Neil, the work does look promising. '

Neil Roy is a well-known actor and superstar in India. His secretary Mr Tandon comes to meet him on a regular Monday morning. 'Good morning Neil , how are you this morning.? Neil replies 'Very well Mr Tandon .'Mr Tandon then enquires about the party Neil attended 'How was the party last night Neil?' Neil replies with a smile it was okay you know I dont much like attending such parties much. ' Mr Tandon says 'Well Neil you know as a superstar you are expected to attend such parties. ' Neil says to Mr Tandon 'Yes and I'm counting on you for all this. Mr Tandon happily 'Certainly Sir Neil then asks about his schedule 'So Mr Tandon what is my schedule for today for today?' Mr Tandon goes on 'Sir you have the shoot at 11 pm for Reena's movie , thereafter they are also having a nice time a get together for lunch on the set for the success of the film's first look. Neil 'Oh that should be fine what next?' Mr Tandon goes on 'Thereafter you have a shoot for Entertainment production company 'Oh Mr Tandon please shift that film shoot further for a while .I'mnptenjoyi g this particular shoot and I   feel we should shift this film further and start working more on Sheena's father's film . This film is going very well and I'm having a very positive feeling of this film. Mr Tandon 'As you wish Neil, the work does look promising. '

Neil Roy is a well-known actor and superstar in India. His secretary Mr Tandon comes to meet him on a regular Monday morning. 'Good morning Neil , how are you this morning.? Neil replies 'Very well Mr Tandon .'Mr Tandon then enquires about the party Neil attended 'How was the party last night Neil?' Neil replies with a smile it was okay you know I dont much like attending such parties much. ' Mr Tandon says 'Well Neil you know as a superstar you are expected to attend such parties. ' Neil says to Mr Tandon 'Yes and I'm counting on you for all this. Mr Tandon happily 'Certainly Sir Neil then asks about his schedule 'So Mr Tandon what is my schedule for today for today?' Mr Tandon goes on 'Sir you have the shoot at 11 pm for Reena's movie , thereafter they are also having a nice time a get together for lunch on the set for the success of the film's first look. Neil 'Oh that should be fine what next?' Mr Tandon goes on 'Thereafter you have a shoot for Entertainment production company 'Oh Mr Tandon please shift that film shoot further for a while .I'mnptenjoyi g this particular shoot and I feel we should shift this film further and start working more on Sheena's father's film . This film is going very well and I'm having a very positive feeling of this film. Mr Tandon 'As you wish Neil, the work does look promising. '

Neil Roy is a well-known actor and superstar in India. His secretary Mr Tandon comes to meet him on a regular Monday morning. 'Good morning Neil , how are you this morning.? Neil replies 'Very well Mr Tandon .'Mr Tandon then enquires about the party Neil attended 'How was the party last night Neil?' Neil replies with a smile it was okay you know I dont much like attending such parties much. ' Mr Tandon says 'Well Neil you know as a superstar you are expected to attend such parties. ' Neil says to Mr Tandon 'Yes and I'm counting on you for all this. Mr Tandon happily 'Certainly Sir Neil then asks about his schedule 'So Mr Tandon what is my schedule for today for today?' Mr Tandon goes on 'Sir you have the shoot at 11 pm for Reena's movie , thereafter they are also having a nice time a get together for lunch on the set for the success of the film's first look. Neil 'Oh that should be fine what next?' Mr Tandon goes on 'Thereafter you have a shoot for Entertainment production company 'Oh Mr Tandon please shift that film shoot further for a while .I'mnptenjoyi g this particular shoot and I feel we should shift this film further and start working more on Sheena's father's film . This film is going very well and I'm having a very positive feeling of this film. Mr Tandon 'As you wish Neil, the work does look promising. '

Neil Roy is a well-known actor and superstar in India. His secretary Mr Tandon comes to meet him on a regular Monday morning. 'Good morning Neil , how are you this morning.? Neil replies 'Very well Mr Tandon .'Mr Tandon then enquires about the party Neil attended 'How was the party last night Neil?' Neil replies with a smile it was okay you know I dont much like attending such parties much. ' Mr Tandon says 'Well Neil you know as a superstar you are expected to attend such parties. ' Neil says to Mr Tandon 'Yes and I'm counting on you for all this. Mr Tandon happily 'Certainly Sir Neil then asks about his schedule 'So Mr Tandon what is my schedule for today for today?' Mr Tandon goes on 'Sir you have the shoot at 11 pm for Reena's movie , thereafter they are also having a nice time a get together for lunch on the set for the success of the film's first look. Neil 'Oh that should be fine what next?' Mr Tandon goes on 'Thereafter you have a shoot for Entertainment production company 'Oh Mr Tandon please shift that film shoot further for a while .I'mnptenjoyi g this particular shoot and I   feel we   should shift this film   further and   start working more on Sheena's father's film . This film is going very well and I'm having a very positive feeling of this film. Mr Tandon 'As you wish Neil, the work does look promising. '

Neil Roy is a well-known actor and superstar in India. His secretary Mr Tandon comes to meet him on a regular Monday morning. 'Good morning Neil , how are you this morning.? Neil replies 'Very well Mr Tandon .'Mr Tandon then enquires about the party Neil attended 'How was the party last night Neil?' Neil replies with a smile it was okay you know I dont much like attending such parties much. ' Mr Tandon says 'Well Neil you know as a superstar you are expected to attend such parties. ' Neil says to Mr Tandon 'Yes and I'm counting on you for all this. Mr Tandon happily 'Certainly Sir   Neil then asks about his schedule 'So Mr Tandon what is my schedule for today for today?' Mr Tandon goes on 'Sir you have the shoot at 11 pm for Reena's movie , thereafter they are also having a nice time a get together for lunch on the set for the success of the film's first look. Neil 'Oh that should be fine what next?' Mr Tandon goes on 'Thereafter you have a shoot for Entertainment production company 'Oh Mr Tandon please shift that film shoot further for a while .I'mnptenjoyi g this particular shoot and I feel we should shift this film further and start working more on Sheena's father's film . This film is going very well and I'm having a very positive feeling of this film. Mr Tandon 'As you wish Neil, the work does look promising. '

Neil Roy is a well-known actor and superstar in India. His secretary Mr Tandon comes to meet him on a regular Monday morning. 'Good morning Neil , how are you this morning.? Neil replies 'Very well Mr Tandon .'Mr Tandon then enquires about the party Neil attended 'How was the party last night Neil?' Neil replies with a smile it was okay you know I dont much like attending such parties much. ' Mr Tandon says 'Well Neil you know as a superstar you are expected to attend such parties. ' Neil says to Mr Tandon 'Yes and I'm counting on you for all this. Mr Tandon happily 'Certainly Sir Neil then asks about his schedule 'So Mr Tandon what is my schedule for today for today?' Mr Tandon goes on 'Sir you have the shoot at 11 pm for Reena's movie , thereafter they are also having a nice time a get together for lunch on the set for the success of the film's first look. Neil 'Oh that should be fine what next?' Mr Tandon goes on 'Thereafter you have a shoot for Entertainment production company 'Oh Mr Tandon please shift that film shoot further for a while .I'mnptenjoyi g this particular shoot and I feel we should shift this film further and start working more on Sheena's father's film . This film is going very well and I'm having a very positive feeling of this film. Mr Tandon 'As you wish Neil, the work does look promising. '

Neil Roy is a well-known actor and superstar in India. His secretary Mr Tandon comes to meet him on a regular Monday morning. 'Good morning Neil , how are you this morning.? Neil replies 'Very well Mr Tandon .'Mr Tandon then enquires about the party Neil attended 'How was the party last night Neil?' Neil replies with a smile it was okay you know I dont much like attending such parties much. ' Mr Tandon says 'Well Neil you know as a superstar you are expected to attend such parties. ' Neil says to Mr Tandon 'Yes and I'm counting on you for all this. Mr Tandon happily 'Certainly Sir Neil then asks about his schedule 'So Mr Tandon what is my schedule for today for today?' Mr Tandon goes on 'Sir you have the shoot at 11 pm for Reena's movie , thereafter they are also having a nice time a get together for lunch on the set for the success of the film's first look. Neil 'Oh that should be fine what next?' Mr Tandon goes on 'Thereafter you have a shoot for Entertainment production company 'Oh Mr Tandon please shift that film shoot further for a while .I'mnptenjoyi g this particular shoot and I feel we should shift this film further and start working more on Sheena's father's film . This film is going very well and I'm having a very positive feeling of this film. Mr Tandon 'As you wish Neil, the work does look promising. '

Neil Roy is a well-known actor and superstar in

India. His secretary Mr Tandon comes to meet him on a regular Monday morning. 'Good morning Neil , how are you this morning.? Neil replies 'Very well Mr Tandon .'Mr Tandon then enquires about the party Neil attended 'How was the party last night Neil?' Neil replies with a smile it was okay you know I dont much like attending such parties much. ' Mr Tandon says 'Well Neil you know as a superstar you are expected to attend such parties. ' Neil says to Mr Tandon 'Yes and I'm counting on you for all this. Mr Tandon happily 'Certainly Sir Neil then asks about his schedule 'So Mr Tandon what is my schedule for today for today?' Mr Tandon goes on 'Sir you have the shoot at 11 pm for Reena's movie , thereafter they are also having a nice time a get together for lunch on the set for the success of the film's first look. Neil 'Oh that should be fine what next?' Mr Tandon goes on 'Thereafter you have a shoot for Entertainment production company 'Oh Mr Tandon please shift that film shoot further for a while .I'mnptenjoyi g this particular shoot and I feel we should shift this film further and start working more on Sheena's father's film . This film is going very well and I'm having a very positive feeling of this film. Mr Tandon 'As you wish Neil, the work does look promising. '
Neil Roy is a well-known actor and superstar in India. His secretary Mr Tandon comes to meet him on a regular Monday morning. 'Good morning Neil , how are you this morning.? Neil replies 'Very well Mr Tandon .'Mr Tandon then enquires about the party Neil attended 'How was the party last night Neil?' Neil

replies with a smile it was okay you know I dont much like attending such parties much. ' Mr Tandon says 'Well Neil you know as a superstar you are expected to attend such parties. ' Neil says to Mr Tandon 'Yes and I'm counting on you for all this. Mr Tandon happily 'Certainly Sir Neil then asks about his schedule 'So Mr Tandon what is my schedule for today for today?' Mr Tandon goes on 'Sir you have the shoot at 11 pm for Reena's movie , thereafter they are also having a nice time a get together for lunch on the set for the success of the film's first look. Neil 'Oh that should be fine what next?' Mr Tandon goes on 'Thereafter you have a shoot for Entertainment production company 'Oh Mr Tandon please shift that film shoot further for a while .I'mnptenjoyi g this particular shoot and I feel we should shift this film further and start working more on Sheena's father's film . This film is going very well and I'm having a very positive feeling of this film. Mr Tandon 'As you wish Neil, the work does look promising. '

Neil Roy is a well-known actor and superstar in India. His secretary Mr Tandon comes to meet him on a regular Monday morning. 'Good morning Neil , how are you this morning.? Neil replies 'Very well Mr Tandon .'Mr Tandon then enquires about the party Neil attended 'How was the party last night Neil?' Neil replies with a smile it was okay you know I dont much like attending such parties much. ' Mr Tandon says 'Well Neil you know as a superstar you are expected to attend such parties. ' Neil says to Mr Tandon 'Yes and I'm counting on you for all this. Mr

Tandon happily 'Certainly Sir   Neil then asks about his schedule 'So Mr Tandon what is my schedule for today for today?' Mr Tandon goes on 'Sir you have the shoot at 11 pm for Reena's movie , thereafter they are also having a nice time   a get together for lunch on the set for the success of the film's first look. Neil 'Oh that should be fine what next?' Mr Tandon goes on 'Thereafter you have a shoot for Entertainment production company 'Oh Mr Tandon please shift that film shoot further for a while .I'mnptenjoyi g this particular shoot and I feel we   should shift this film further and start working more on Sheena's father's film . This film is going very well and I'm having a very positive feeling of this film. Mr Tandon 'As you wish Neil, the work does look promising. '

Repetition of Chapter 1 Ignore

Neil Roy is a well-known actor and superstar in India. His secretary Mr Tandon comes to meet him on a regular Monday morning. 'Good morning Neil , how are you this morning.? Neil replies 'Very well Mr Tandon .'Mr Tandon then enquires about the party Neil attended 'How was the party last night Neil?' Neil replies with a smile it was okay you know I dont much like attending such parties much. ' Mr Tandon says 'Well Neil you know as a superstar you are expected to attend such parties. ' Neil says to Mr Tandon 'Yes and I'm counting on you for all this. Mr Tandon happily 'Certainly Sir Neil then asks about his schedule 'So Mr Tandon what is my schedule for today for today?' Mr Tandon goes on 'Sir you have the shoot at 11 pm for Reena's movie , thereafter they are also having a nice time a get together for lunch on the set for the success of the film's first look. Neil 'Oh that should be fine what next?' Mr Tandon goes on 'Thereafter you have a shoot for Entertainment production company 'Oh Mr Tandon please shift that film shoot further for a while .I'mnptenjoyi g this particular shoot and I feel we should shift this film further and start working more on Sheena's father's film . This film is going very well and I'm having a very positive feeling of this film. Mr Tandon 'As you wish Neil, the work does look promising. '
is first time writer Kavita Thomas.Hope the readers like

first official effort.Neil Roy is a well-known actor and superstar in India. His secretary Mr Tandon comes to meet him on a regular Monday morning. 'Good morning Neil , how are you this morning.? Neil replies 'Very well Mr Tandon .'Mr Tandon then enquires about the party Neil attended 'How was the party last night Neil?' Neil replies with a smile it was okay you know I dont much like attending such parties much. ' Mr Tandon says 'Well Neil you know as a superstar you are expected to attend such parties. ' Neil says to Mr Tandon 'Yes and I'm counting on you for all this. Mr Tandon happily 'Certainly Sir Neil then asks about his schedule 'So Mr Tandon what is my schedule for today for today?' Mr Tandon goes on 'Sir you have the shoot at 11 pm for Reena's movie , thereafter they are also having a nice time a get together for lunch on the set for the success of the film's first look. Neil 'Oh that should be fine what next?' Mr Tandon goes on 'Thereafter you have a shoot for Entertainment production company 'Oh Mr Tandon please shift that film shoot further for a while .I'mnptenjoyi g this particular shoot and I feel we should shift this film further and start working more on Sheena's father's film . This film is going very well and I'm having a very positive feeling of this film. Mr Tandon 'As you wish Neil, the work does look promising. '

Neil Roy is a well-known actor and superstar in India. His secretary Mr Tandon comes to meet him on a regular Monday morning. 'Good morning Neil , how are you this morning.? Neil replies 'Very well Mr Tandon .'Mr Tandon then enquires about the party

Neil attended 'How was the party last night Neil?' Neil replies with a smile it was okay you know I dont much like attending such parties much. ' Mr Tandon says 'Well Neil you know as a superstar you are expected to attend such parties. ' Neil says to Mr Tandon 'Yes and I'm counting on you for all this. Mr Tandon happily 'Certainly Sir Neil then asks about his schedule 'So Mr Tandon what is my schedule for today for today?' Mr Tandon goes on 'Sir you have the shoot at 11 pm for Reena's movie , thereafter they are also having a nice time a get together for lunch on the set for the success of the film's first look. Neil 'Oh that should be fine what next?' Mr Tandon goes on 'Thereafter you have a shoot for Entertainment production company 'Oh Mr Tandon please shift that film shoot further for a while .I'mnptenjoyi g this particular shoot and I feel we should shift this film further and start working more on Sheena's father's film . This film is going very well and I'm having a very positive feeling of this film. Mr Tandon 'As you wish Neil, the work does look promising. '

Neil Roy is a well-known actor and superstar in India. His secretary Mr Tandon comes to meet him on a regular Monday morning. 'Good morning Neil , how are you this morning.? Neil replies 'Very well Mr Tandon .'Mr Tandon then enquires about the party Neil attended 'How was the party last night Neil?' Neil replies with a smile it was okay you know I dont much like attending such parties much. ' Mr Tandon says 'Well Neil you know as a superstar you are expected to attend such parties. ' Neil says to Mr

Tandon 'Yes and I'm counting on you for all this. Mr Tandon happily 'Certainly Sir Neil then asks about his schedule 'So Mr Tandon what is my schedule for today for today?' Mr Tandon goes on 'Sir you have the shoot at 11 pm for Reena's movie , thereafter they are also having a nice time a get together for lunch on the set for the success of the film's first look. Neil 'Oh that should be fine what next?' Mr Tandon goes on 'Thereafter you have a shoot for Entertainment production company 'Oh Mr Tandon please shift that film shoot further for a while .I'mnptenjoyi g this particular shoot and I feel we should shift this film further and start working more on Sheena's father's film . This film is going very well and I'm having a very positive feeling of this film. Mr Tandon 'As you wish Neil, the work does look promising. '

Neil Roy is a well-known actor and superstar in India. His secretary Mr Tandon comes to meet him on a regular Monday morning. 'Good morning Neil , how are you this morning.? Neil replies 'Very well Mr Tandon .'Mr Tandon then enquires about the party Neil attended 'How was the party last night Neil?' Neil replies with a smile it was okay you know I dont much like attending such parties much. ' Mr Tandon says 'Well Neil you know as a superstar you are expected to attend such parties. ' Neil says to Mr Tandon 'Yes and I'm counting on you for all this. Mr Tandon happily 'Certainly Sir Neil then asks about his schedule 'So Mr Tandon what is my schedule for today for today?' Mr Tandon goes on 'Sir you have the shoot at 11 pm for Reena's movie , thereafter they are also having a nice time a get together for lunch on the set for the success of the film's first look. Neil 'Oh that should be fine what next?' Mr Tandon goes on 'Thereafter you have a shoot for Entertainment production company 'Oh Mr Tandon please shift that film shoot further for a while .I'mnptenjoyi g this particular shoot and I feel we should shift this film further and start working more on Sheena's father's film . This film is going very well and I'm having a very positive feeling of this film. Mr Tandon 'As you wish Neil, the work does look promising. '

Neil Roy is a well-known actor and superstar in India. His secretary Mr Tandon comes to meet him on a regular Monday morning. 'Good morning Neil , how are you this morning.? Neil replies 'Very well Mr Tandon .'Mr Tandon then enquires about the party Neil attended 'How was the party last night Neil?' Neil replies with a smile it was okay you know I dont much like attending such parties much. ' Mr Tandon says 'Well Neil you know as a superstar you are expected to attend such parties. ' Neil says to Mr Tandon 'Yes and I'm counting on you for all this. Mr Tandon happily 'Certainly Sir Neil then asks about his schedule 'So Mr Tandon what is my schedule for today for today?' Mr Tandon goes on 'Sir you have the shoot at 11 pm for Reena's movie , thereafter they are also having a nice time a get together for lunch on the set for the success of the film's first look. Neil 'Oh that should be fine what next?' Mr Tandon goes on 'Thereafter you have a shoot for Entertainment production company 'Oh Mr

Tandon please shift that film shoot further for a while .I'mnptenjoyi g this particular shoot and I feel we should shift this film further and start working more on Sheena's father's film . This film is going very well and I'm having a very positive feeling of this film. Mr Tandon 'As you wish Neil, the work does look promising. '

Neil Roy is a well-known actor and superstar in India. His secretary Mr Tandon comes to meet him on a regular Monday morning. 'Good morning Neil , how are you this morning.? Neil replies 'Very well Mr Tandon .'Mr Tandon then enquires about the party Neil attended 'How was the party last night Neil?' Neil replies with a smile it was okay you know I dont much like attending such parties much. ' Mr Tandon says 'Well Neil you know as a superstar you are expected to attend such parties. ' Neil says to Mr Tandon 'Yes and I'm counting on you for all this. Mr Tandon happily 'Certainly Sir Neil then asks about his schedule 'So Mr Tandon what is my schedule for today for today?' Mr Tandon goes on 'Sir you have the shoot at 11 pm for Reena's movie , thereafter they are also having a nice time a get together for lunch on the set for the success of the film's first look. Neil 'Oh that should be fine what next?' Mr Tandon goes on 'Thereafter you have a shoot for Entertainment production company 'Oh Mr Tandon please shift that film shoot further for a while .I'mnptenjoyi g this particular shoot and I feel we should shift this film further and start working more on Sheena's father's film . This film is going very well and I'm having a very positive feeling of this film. Mr Tandon 'As you wish Neil, the work does look promising. '

Neil Roy is a well-known actor and superstar in India. His secretary Mr Tandon comes to meet him on a regular Monday morning. 'Good morning Neil , how are you this morning.? Neil replies 'Very well Mr Tandon .'Mr Tandon then enquires about the party Neil attended 'How was the party last night Neil?' Neil replies with a smile it was okay you know I dont much like attending such parties much. ' Mr Tandon says 'Well Neil you know as a superstar you are expected to attend such parties. ' Neil says to Mr Tandon 'Yes and I'm counting on you for all this. Mr Tandon happily 'Certainly Sir Neil then asks about his schedule 'So Mr Tandon what is my schedule for today for today?' Mr Tandon goes on 'Sir you have the shoot at 11 pm for Reena's movie , thereafter they are also having a nice time a get together for lunch on the set for the success of the film's first look. Neil 'Oh that should be fine what next?' Mr Tandon goes on 'Thereafter you have a shoot for Entertainment production company 'Oh Mr Tandon please shift that film shoot further for a while .I'mnptenjoyi g this particular shoot and I feel we should shift this film further and start working more on Sheena's father's film . This film is going very well and I'm having a very positive feeling of this film. Mr Tandon 'As you wish Neil, the work does look promising. '

Neil Roy is a well-known actor and superstar in India. His secretary Mr Tandon comes to meet him on a regular Monday morning. 'Good morning Neil , how are you this morning.? Neil replies 'Very well Mr Tandon .'Mr Tandon then enquires about the party Neil attended 'How was the party last night Neil?' Neil replies with a smile it was okay you know I dont much like attending such parties much. ' Mr Tandon says 'Well Neil you know as a superstar you are expected to attend such parties. ' Neil says to Mr Tandon 'Yes and I'm counting on you for all this. Mr Tandon happily 'Certainly Sir Neil then asks about his schedule 'So Mr Tandon what is my schedule for today for today?' Mr Tandon goes on 'Sir you have the shoot at 11 pm for Reena's movie , thereafter they are also having a nice time a get together for lunch on the set for the success of the film's first look. Neil 'Oh that should be fine what next?' Mr Tandon goes on 'Thereafter you have a shoot for Entertainment production company 'Oh Mr Tandon please shift that film shoot further for a while .I'mnptenjoyi g this particular shoot and I feel we should shift this film further and start working more on Sheena's father's film . This film is going very well and I'm having a very positive feeling of this film. Mr Tandon 'As you wish Neil, the work does look promising. '

Neil Roy is a well-known actor and superstar in India. His secretary Mr Tandon comes to meet him on a regular Monday morning. 'Good morning Neil , how are you this morning.? Neil replies 'Very well Mr Tandon .'Mr Tandon then enquires about the party Neil attended 'How was the party last night Neil?' Neil replies with a smile it was okay you know I dont much like attending such parties much. ' Mr Tandon says 'Well Neil you know as a superstar you are expected to attend such parties. ' Neil says to Mr Tandon 'Yes and I'm counting on you for all this. Mr Tandon happily 'Certainly Sir Neil then asks about his schedule 'So Mr Tandon what is my schedule for today for today?' Mr Tandon goes on 'Sir you have the shoot at 11 pm for Reena's movie , thereafter they are also having a nice time a get together for lunch on the set for the success of the film's first look. Neil 'Oh that should be fine what next?' Mr Tandon goes on 'Thereafter you have a shoot for Entertainment production company 'Oh Mr Tandon please shift that film shoot further for a while .I'mnptenjoyi g this particular shoot and I feel we should shift this film further and start working more on Sheena's father's film . This film is going very well and I'm having a very positive feeling of this film. Mr Tandon 'As you wish Neil, the work does look promising. '

Neil Roy is a well-known actor and superstar in India. His secretary Mr Tandon comes to meet him on a regular Monday morning. 'Good morning Neil , how are you this morning.? Neil replies 'Very well Mr Tandon .'Mr Tandon then enquires about the party Neil attended 'How was the party last night Neil?' Neil replies with a smile it was okay you know I dont much like attending such parties much. ' Mr Tandon says 'Well Neil you know as a superstar you are expected to attend such parties. ' Neil says to Mr Tandon 'Yes and I'm counting on you for all this. Mr Tandon happily 'Certainly Sir Neil then asks about his schedule 'So Mr Tandon what is my schedule for today for today?' Mr Tandon goes on 'Sir you have the shoot at 11 pm for Reena's movie , thereafter they are also having a nice time a get together for lunch on the set for the success of the film's first look. Neil 'Oh that should be fine what next?' Mr Tandon goes on 'Thereafter you have a shoot for Entertainment production company 'Oh Mr Tandon please shift that film shoot further for a while .I'mnptenjoyi g this particular shoot and I feel we should shift this film further and start working more on Sheena's father's film . This film is going very well and I'm having a very positive feeling of this film. Mr Tandon 'As you wish Neil, the work does look promising. '

Neil Roy is a well-known actor and superstar in India. His secretary Mr Tandon comes to meet him on a regular Monday morning. 'Good morning Neil , how are you this morning.? Neil replies 'Very well Mr Tandon .'Mr Tandon then enquires about the party Neil attended 'How was the party last night Neil?' Neil replies with a smile it was okay you know I dont much like attending such parties much. ' Mr Tandon says 'Well Neil you know as a superstar you are expected to attend such parties. ' Neil says to Mr Tandon 'Yes and I'm counting on you for all this. Mr Tandon happily 'Certainly Sir Neil then asks about his schedule 'So Mr Tandon what is my schedule for today for today?' Mr Tandon goes on 'Sir you have the shoot at 11 pm for Reena's movie , thereafter they are also having a nice time a get together for lunch on the set for the success of the film's first look. Neil 'Oh that should be fine what next?' Mr Tandon goes on 'Thereafter you have a shoot for Entertainment production company 'Oh Mr Tandon please shift that film shoot further for a while .I'mnptenjoyi g this particular shoot and I feel we should shift this film further and start working more on Sheena's father's film . This film is going very well and I'm having a very positive feeling of this film. Mr Tandon 'As you wish Neil, the work does look promising. '

Neil Roy is a well-known actor and superstar in India. His secretary Mr Tandon comes to meet him on a regular Monday morning. 'Good morning Neil , how are you this morning.? Neil replies 'Very well Mr Tandon .'Mr Tandon then enquires about the party Neil attended 'How was the party last night Neil?' Neil replies with a smile it was okay you know I dont much like attending such parties much. ' Mr Tandon says 'Well Neil you know as a superstar you are expected to attend such parties. ' Neil says to Mr Tandon 'Yes and I'm counting on you for all this. Mr Tandon happily 'Certainly Sir Neil then asks about his schedule 'So Mr Tandon what is my schedule for today for today?' Mr Tandon goes on 'Sir you have the shoot at 11 pm for Reena's movie , thereafter they are also having a nice time a get together for lunch on the set for the success of the film's first look. Neil 'Oh that should be fine what next?' Mr Tandon goes on 'Thereafter you have a shoot for Entertainment production company 'Oh Mr Tandon please shift that film shoot further for a while .I'mnptenjoyi g this particular shoot and I feel we should shift this film further and start working more on Sheena's father's film . This film is going very well and I'm having a very positive feeling of this film. Mr Tandon 'As you wish Neil, the work does look promising. '

Neil Roy is a well-known actor and superstar in India. His secretary Mr Tandon comes to meet him on a regular Monday morning. 'Good morning Neil , how are you this morning.? Neil replies 'Very well Mr Tandon .'Mr Tandon then enquires about the party Neil attended 'How was the party last night Neil?' Neil replies with a smile it was okay you know I dont much like attending such parties much. ' Mr Tandon says 'Well Neil you know as a superstar you are expected to attend such parties. ' Neil says to Mr Tandon 'Yes and I'm counting on you for all this. Mr Tandon happily 'Certainly Sir Neil then asks about his schedule 'So Mr Tandon what is my schedule for today for today?' Mr Tandon goes on 'Sir you have the shoot at 11 pm for Reena's movie , thereafter they are also having a nice time a get together for lunch on the set for the success of the film's first look. Neil 'Oh that should be fine what next?' Mr Tandon goes on 'Thereafter you have a shoot for Entertainment production company 'Oh Mr Tandon please shift that film shoot further for a while .I'mnptenjoyi g this particular shoot and I feel we should shift this film further and start working more on Sheena's father's film . This film is going very well and I'm having a very positive feeling of this film. Mr Tandon 'As you wish Neil, the work does look promising. '

Neil Roy is a well-known actor and superstar in

India. His secretary Mr Tandon comes to meet him on a regular Monday morning. 'Good morning Neil , how are you this morning.? Neil replies 'Very well Mr Tandon .'Mr Tandon then enquires about the party Neil attended 'How was the party last night Neil?' Neil replies with a smile it was okay you know I dont much like attending such parties much. ' Mr Tandon says 'Well Neil you know as a superstar you are expected to attend such parties. ' Neil says to Mr Tandon 'Yes and I'm counting on you for all this. Mr Tandon happily 'Certainly Sir Neil then asks about his schedule 'So Mr Tandon what is my schedule for today for today?' Mr Tandon goes on 'Sir you have the shoot at 11 pm for Reena's movie , thereafter they are also having a nice time a get together for lunch on the set for the success of the film's first look. Neil 'Oh that should be fine what next?' Mr Tandon goes on 'Thereafter you have a shoot for Entertainment production company 'Oh Mr Tandon please shift that film shoot further for a while .I'mnptenjoyi g this particular shoot and I feel we should shift this film further and start working more on Sheena's father's film . This film is going very well and I'm having a very positive feeling of this film. Mr Tandon 'As you wish Neil, the work does look promising. '

Neil Roy is a well-known actor and superstar in India. His secretary Mr Tandon comes to meet him on a regular Monday morning. 'Good morning Neil , how are you this morning.? Neil replies 'Very well Mr Tandon .'Mr Tandon then enquires about the party Neil attended 'How was the party last night Neil?' Neil replies with a smile it was okay you know I dont much like attending such parties much. ' Mr Tandon says 'Well Neil you know as a superstar you are expected to attend such parties. ' Neil says to Mr Tandon 'Yes and I'm counting on you for all this. Mr Tandon happily 'Certainly Sir Neil then asks about his schedule 'So Mr Tandon what is my schedule for today for today?' Mr Tandon goes on 'Sir you have the shoot at 11 pm for Reena's movie , thereafter they are also having a nice time a get together for lunch on the set for the success of the film's first look. Neil 'Oh that should be fine what next?' Mr Tandon goes on 'Thereafter you have a shoot for Entertainment production company 'Oh Mr Tandon please shift that film shoot further for a while .I'mnptenjoyi g this particular shoot and I feel we should shift this film further and start working more on Sheena's father's film . This film is going very well and I'm having a very positive feeling of this film. Mr Tandon 'As you wish Neil, the work does look promising. '

Neil Roy is a well-known actor and superstar in India. His secretary Mr Tandon comes to meet him on a regular Monday morning. 'Good morning Neil , how are you this morning.? Neil replies 'Very well Mr Tandon .'Mr Tandon then enquires about the party Neil attended 'How was the party last night Neil?' Neil replies with a smile it was okay you know I dont much like attending such parties much. ' Mr Tandon says 'Well Neil you know as a superstar you are expected to attend such parties. ' Neil says to Mr Tandon 'Yes and I'm counting on you for all this. Mr

Tandon happily 'Certainly Sir   Neil then asks about his schedule 'So Mr Tandon what is my schedule for today for today?' Mr Tandon goes on 'Sir you have the shoot at 11 pm for Reena's movie , thereafter they are also having a nice time a get together for lunch on the set for the success of the film's first look. Neil 'Oh that should be fine what next?' Mr Tandon goes on 'Thereafter you have a shoot for Entertainment production company 'Oh Mr Tandon please shift that film shoot further for a while .I'mnptenjoyi g this particular shoot and I feel we should shift this film further and start working more on Sheena's father's film . This film is going very well and I'm having a very positive feeling of this film. Mr Tandon 'As you wish Neil, the work does look promising. '

Chapter 2

Sheena Soni is a well-known actress who is also acting in this particular film with Neil. Sheena drops in to meet Neil whom she is in a relationship with .'Hello Neil , How are things going?' Neil replies ' Hello sheena, why didn't you come to the party last night?' Sheena says lazily' Oh my shoot last evening went on till late in the night, so post wrap up things had to be taken care of and so I had to skip theparty . Sheena to Neil 'Seems like you enjoyed the party?' Neil smiling 'Oh come off it Sheena, you know how I feel of such parties. Can I drop you to your shoot.?' I'm on my way to Reena's shoot, Sheena gladly replies 'oh yes I would get to spend some time with you, my driver can follow.' In the afternoon Sheena joins in Reena's lunch get together with Neil, Sheena arrives 'Hello everyone are you'll done with today's shoot. Reena says 'Hello Sheena, this is a surprise, welcome to our party.Yes, the shoot is over it was a bit hectic for everyone today. What will you have , please make yourself comfortable. Sheena replies 'Thankyou Reena ' .I will and goes on to meet the others.Neil takes Sheena to a side and tells her a little annoyed, 'Sheena why did you wear this outfit for this party today. I've told you to not wear such revealing clothes. Sheena replies 'oh come onNeil you've got to change this outlook of yours, an actress has to look glamorous all the time and walks away from him., while Neil looks on agitated.

Among other guests walks in Sonia Roy an upcoming model and daughter of a producer who has just come into town. She walks in with a friend of hers Ron. Reena comes to welcome Sonia"Hello Sonia welcome to our small get together Sonia she says .Sonia replies ' Hello Reena I'mglad that your upcoming film is shaping up well, it's my pleasure to be a part of your celebrations .' Reena enquires about Mr Roy , Sonia's father ' How's Mr Roy Sonia.' Sonia very pleased replies ' Very well Reena , he's busy with his production work for his first upcoming film. Reena suddenly asks Sonia 'Aren't you going to work in your father's film. Reena suddenly asks Sonia 'Aren't you going to work in your father's film? to which Sonia replies hesitatingly 'Well this is something I've got to see, not as of now!' Reena updates Sonia about the rumours in the media about Sonia acting in the film to which Sonia replies a bit annoyed ' Oh Reena , you know the media, they're just looking out for a news. Sonia then introduces Ron who had also come into town and is also a model, 'Reena meet my friend and colleague Ron , he's just flown in with me for the same modelling assignment.'Hello Ron' I know him although this is the first time we meet , isn't it Ron?' Toon replies to Reena 'No Reena I've met you at a party before of an advertising agency . Reena being apologetic ' oh I'm sorry Ron , I hardly remember all this please enjoy the party and make yourself comfortable. Ron replies gladly 'Certainly Reena.' Reena then tells Sonia , Oh' here cones Sheena let me introduce you to her. Reena introducing Sonia to Sheena says 'Sheena this is Sonia , she's an upcoming model and has just come to town.' Sheena greats Sonia 'Hello Sonia are you enjoying the y?' Sonia replies smiling 'Yes and asks Sheena if she is part of the film as well. Sheena replies oh, no Sonia I'm not working in this film but a close friend of mine is a part of this film.' Reena adds further 'Sheena Soni is a producer 's daughter herself to which Sheena replies 'Oh is that so?' Reena tells Sheena 'Yes , her father Mr Roy has just got into production with his upcoming film.' Sheena tells Sonia 'Well Sonia I hope your father does well with his new project.' Reena tells Sheena that Sonia is even thinking of working in her father's film, to which Sheena says turning to Sonia 'Is that so Sonia?' and adds a bit proudly 'But do you have any experience in acting?' A good model may not be a good actress and walks away sarcastically . Sonia asks Reena a bit upset 'What was that all about Reena?' Reena tells Sonia to not bother about what Sheena said, 'Let it be Sonia, how does anything she say affect you in any way. Reena thenmoveson to interact with the other guests and while Sonia looks around she comes across Neil who was standing on the other side upset with Sheena. She feels attracted towards him, an attraction that even she couldn't understand. Suddenly Ron comes to Sonia and tells her that they've been called for a meeting regarding their assignment. Sonia quickly says 'Let's go Ron ' and they walk towards Reena to tell her they were leaving. While walking towards Reena Sonia keeps looking at Neil. Neil realises that Sonia was looking at him and he looks at her too, a bit surprised and wondering about Sonia.

Ron leaves Sonia to her room in the evening. He says 'I like this assignment and we are going to have a great time on this project.' Sonia nods with a slight smile.Ronasks sonia'What's it Sonia, you seem to be preoccupied , infact you were quiet all evening .' Sonia a bit hesitatingly says 'Oh nothing Ron, it's just one of those days.Ron tells her 'We've not been able to spend much time lately Sonia.' Sonia tells him 'I know Ron .' Ron then tells her that he is leaving and that he would meet her tomorrow at their photoshoot. Sonia says 'AlrightRon'Good night'. As Ron leaves Sonia's phone rings, it is her father who is calling, he asks her 'How was the day with your assignment Sonia?'

Sonia says ' okay daddy' infact it was an interesting da notices Sonia looking towards him, he remembers that this is the same lady who was staring at him at the party earlier. He also feels an attraction towards her and at the same time she was suddenly called by the makers of by the makers of Sonia's project to get on with the events of the night of the night. Neil goes along with them .

The event is going on and Ron and Sonia have been called to the event to the event . Neil is introduced to Sonia and

Sonia and Ron . They are both very happy aut this is not the first time I'm seeing you Sonia says 'Me too '. They are interrupted by the organisers , while continuing the event further . Ron and Sonia head towards the dinner section . Ron tells Sonia that he is enjoying the evening . Sonia tells him trrrRR444RRrhat she is also having a nice time , and looks at Neil . Neil meanwhile sees Sonia and asks sees Sonia and asks the organisers about Sonia. They tell him that she has come to town especially for the assignment. The event and party is almost over. Neil is anout to leave the party and goes towards the organisers to tell them that he was leaving , he finds Ron and Sonia there and wishes them for their assignment . They wish him good luck with his with his forthcoming projects as well. He tells them 'It was nice meeting you'll both '. Sonia replies 'It was nice meeting you too Mr Neil. ' Neil smiles and says 'Goodnight and leaves the party. Ron leaves Sonia to her hotel . He tells her that he was not only happy with the party with the party but was also glad that he could spend time with her

Sonia tells him that she has not thought about him and their relationship so seriously and asks him also to give her more time to think. She also told him that he should also control himself as she didn't feel as she didn't feel the same about him yet. While Sonia is getting ready for the shoot one morning she gets a call from her father that he is arriving to town by the afternoon flight. She asks him why he didn't inform her. He tells it was a sudden decision as, he wanted to start his first production sooner . She tells him that she would meet him at the airport . Sonia tells Ron that she is leaving for the airport to meet her father. Ron says that he will keep in mind what they discussed and asked her if   she wants him to accompany her to the airport. Sonia says 'No Ron ' please continue with your work .' I 'd like to spend time with my father. ' Ron leaves for the shoot again and while Sonia and while Sonia is about to leave she informs the director that she is leaving as she has to meet her father. Sonia arrives at the airport   to receive her father. She tells her father that she is coming from the shoot. Her father tells her 'Sonia so good to see you '. Sonia replies 'So Daddy is the production going to be earlier than the schedule ?' Her father says 'Yes I want to begin soon as well . How was the party Sonia?' Very well daddy , it was great infact . Her father says "I'm very happy that your project has a good review already. ' He tells her that he is going to his rented house and would like her also to join . She said she would join him soon join him soon. Sonia tells him that she is joining her father at his appartment .Ron tells their assignment is almost over and he will be returning back after its all done. Sonia just smiles , she notices a message from an award function invitation an award function invitation . She joins her father in the evening for dinner at the appartment. Her father mentions   that he was in the process of deciding the cast of

She further asks him about   the film and at that time he tells her that he wants her to act in his film as her project was also doing well. She tells him that she is not interested in acting in his film or for any other film. Her father asks her to think again and she says she is not interested. Sonia's assignment is nearing completion .Ron tells Sonia that he is going to be with her father for some more time. She tells him that she will leave as well after their work and not be around for very long as her father will be around there for some more tim jie for his production work. While Sonia's father 's production company begins preparation and deciding on the cast .Sonia completes work on her assignment and tells Ron that and tells Ron that she enjoyed working with him. 'Ron you know I had a nice time shooting with you, regardless of our personal relationship. Ron says 'I know Sonia .I enjoyed working with you. ' He tells her tha

Space of Chapter 3

Ron

Chapter 3

Sonia says ' okay   daddy' infact it was an interesting da notices Sonia looking towards him, he remembers that this is the   same lady who was staring at him at the party earlier. He also feels an attraction towards her   and at the   same time she was wondering about the look that Sonia had on her face. He is suddenly called by the makers of by the makers of Sonia's project to get on with the events of the night of the night. Neil goes along with them .

The   event is going on and Ron and Sonia   have been called to the event   to   the   event . Neil   is introduced to Sonia and Sonia and Ron . They are both very happy aut this is not the first time I'm seeing you Sonia says 'Me   too '. They are interrupted by the organisers , while continuing the event further . Ron and Sonia   head towards the dinner section   . Ron tells Sonia   that he is   enjoying the evening . Sonia tells him that she is also having a nice time , and looks at Neil . Neil meanwhile sees Sonia and asks   sees Sonia and asks the organisers about Sonia. They   tell him that she   has come to   town especially for the assignment. The event and party is almost over. Neil is anout to leave the party and goes towards the organisers to tell them that he was leaving , he finds Ron and Sonia there and wishes them for their assignment . They wish him good luck with his with his forthcoming projects as well. He tells them 'It was nice meeting you'll both '. Sonia replies 'It was nice meeting you too Mr Neil. ' Neil smiles and says 'Goodnight and leaves the party. Ron leaves Sonia to her hotel . He tells her that he was not only happy with the party with the party but was also glad that he could spend time with her

Sonia tells him that she has not thought about him and their relationship so seriously and asks him also to give her more time to think. She also told him that he should also control himself as she didn't feel as she didn't feel the same about him yet. While Sonia is getting ready for the shoot one morning she gets a call from her father that he is arriving to town by the afternoon flight. She asks him why he didn't inform her. He tells it was a sudden decision as, he wanted to start his first production sooner . She tells him that she would meet him at the airport . Sonia tells Ron that she is leaving for the airport to meet her father. Ron says that he will keep in mind what they discussed and asked her if she wants him to accompany her to the airport. Sonia says 'No Ron ' please continue with your work .' I 'd like to spend time with my father. ' Ron leaves for the shoot again and while Sonia and while Sonia is about to leave she informs the director that she is leaving as she has to meet her father. Sonia arrives at the airport to receive her father.

She tells her father that she is coming from the shoot. Her father tells her 'Sonia so good to see you '. Sonia replies 'So Daddy is the production going to be earlier than the schedule ?' Her father says 'Yes I want to begin soon as well . How was the party Sonia?' Very well daddy , it was great infact . Her father says "I'm very happy that your project has a good review already. ' He tells her that he is going to his rented house and would like her also to join . She said she would join him soon join him soon. Sonia tells him that she is joining her father at his appartment .Ron tells their assignment is almost over and he will be returning back after its all done. Sonia just smiles , she notices a message from an award function invitation an award function invitation . She joins her father in the evening for dinner at the appartment. Her father mentions that he was in the process of deciding the cast of his first production film.

She further asks him about the film and at that time he tells her that he wants her to act in his film as her project was also doing well. She tells him that she is not interested in acting in his film or for any other film. Her father asks her to think again and she says she is not interested. Sonia's assignment is nearing completion .Ron tells Sonia that he is going to be with her father for some more time. She tells him that she will leave as well after their work and not be around for very long as her father will be around there for some more time for his production work. While Sonia's father 's production company begins preparation and deciding on the cast .Sonia completes work on her assignment and tells Ron that and tells Ron that she enjoyed working with him. 'Ron you know I had a nice time shooting with you, regardless of our personal relationship. Ron says 'I know Sonia .I enjoyed working with you. ' He tells her that he is also invited to the award function that Sonia is invited and asks her to join him so that they could go for the show together. Ron further tells Sonia 'Sonia I intend to leave after the function , 'Oh I see Sonia replies to Ron adding further .Alright Ron let's meet and leave for the function together.

Sonia is getting ready for the function. She tells her father that she will meet him post the function. Her father says 'I hope you won't be too late. Sonia says 'I think it will take a while and I'll be late.

Space of Chapter 3

Ron

Chapter 4

Ron arrives to pickup Sonia 'Hello Sir Ron greets Sonia's father. Mr Roy greets him and asks him if he intends to be there longer to which Ron says 'Oh no Sir, I'll be going back the day after I was just waiting for this function . Sonia and Ron then leave for the function while Ron and Sonia arrive at the function. Neil and Sonia are getting ready to attend the award function . Neil has come over to pickup Sheena. Hello Sheena Neil tells her 'Are you ready to leave?' 'Yes Neil Sheena replies 'How was your shoot?' Sheena asks him about his shoot of their movie together. She further says 'You still have few more days of your shoot, before i join the shoot. Neil says 'Yes sometime more. 'Sheena says in that way I'll be able to spend some more time with you .'Yes Sheena replies Neil.Neil and Sheena arrive at the function. Sheena tells Neil 'The last time I went out with you to Reena's party you didn't like the outfit, I hope you like this one Neil. Neil says 'Well Sheena .'I'm sorry about that day says Sheena. It's okay Neil tells her it's in the past . Sheena says further 'No really I just thought of it now Neil smilesand says' Alright Sheena'. Neil spots Ron and Sonia at the awards function and Sonia notices Neil as well . Sonia smiles at Neil. Sonia keeps looking towards Neil which even Neil. Sonia and Ron are joined by certain common friends. The function begins and Neil happens to get happens to get an award for which Sonia is called on stage. Sonia who was happy with her recognition that she was getting from her assignment says 'Congratulations on receiving this award' to Neil and Neil announces that he is happy to receive this award from Sonia. Sheena is not pleased with this. She asks Neil as soon as possible as he comes to his seat. 'Do you know this Sonia Neil, Yes, Ive met her before replies Neil. Sheena inyerested to know more asks him 'Where and How?' I was invited to her assignment success party remember that party where l was invited as a chief guest, it was their party, Sheena says 'Oh I see and adds further 'She is a pretty lady .Neil replies 'Yes she's very pretty ' and sheena looks at him as Neil looks towards Sonia . Pictures of Neil and Sonia are published in the newspapers .The next day of the award function .Mr Tandon talks of the picture in the paper while Neil takes a look at them as Sheena walks in. Sheena a bit jealous says 'I don't know why the media is giving importance to this importance to this upcoming model along with commenting about you . Neil tells her 'Oh come on Sheena you're being rude, everyone deserves their share of limelight . To which Sheena replies 'So we have a Sonia's fan over here. ' Neil says 'Sheena , come on.'

Sheena says 'Alright come on, let's go. Sonia's father sees the pictures in the newspaper and asks Sonia if she has met Neil before. She says that she met him at their success party. He tells her that their production company company was considering Neil for their film . Sonia says 'Oh , I see .' Do you want to come to my office Sonia. Sonia says 'No daddy I'mmeeting Ron for lunch today as he's leaving tomorrow ' Okay Sonia says her father. So I'll meet you later. Sonia says 'Bye Daddy. ' Sonia meets Ron for lunch .She tells him 'So Ron you have another assignment lined. I hope you enjoy your new work . Yes Sonia Ron says and adds further 'I hope so too. I wish you would also be there with me. ' Sonia tells him 'Well its not like , I'll be away.' I should leave in some time too.' Ron tells her 'Well Sonia thanks for spending the afternoon with me. ' She tells him 'Ron , why don't you join daddy and me for dinner tonight. 'Ron joins Sonia and her father for dinner. Ron tells her father that they've been dating. Sonia's father tells him 'I knew you'll were close. ' But we haven't moved further. 'Ron added as Sonia needs time. 'Ron arrives to pickup Sonia 'Hello Sir Ron greets Sonia's father. Mr Roy greets him and asks him if he intends to be there longer to which Ron says 'Oh no Sir, I'll be going back the day after I was just waiting for this function . Sonia and Ron then leave for the function while Ron and Sonia arrive at the function. Neil and Sonia are getting ready to attend the award function . Neil has come over to pickup Sheena. Hello Sheena Neil tells her 'Are you ready to leave?' 'Yes Neil Sheena replies 'How was your shoot?' Sheena asks him about his shoot of their movie together. She further says 'You still have few more days of your shoot, before i join the shoot. Neil says 'Yes sometime more. 'Sheena says in that way I'll be able to spend some more time with you .'Yes Sheena replies Neil.Neil and Sheena arrive at the function. Sheena tells Neil 'The last time I went out with you to Reena's party you didn't like the outfit, I hope you like this one Neil. Neil says 'Well Sheena .'I'm sorry about that day says Sheena. It's okay Neil tells her it's in the past . Sheena says further 'No really I just thought of it now Neil smilesand says' Alright Sheena'. Neil spots Ron and Sonia at the awards function and Sonia notices Neil as well . Sonia smiles at Neil. Sonia keeps looking towards Neil which even Neil. Sonia and Ron are joined by certain common friends. The function begins and Neil happens to get happens to get an award for which Sonia is called on stage. Sonia who was happy with her recognition that she was getting from her assignment says

'Congratulations on receiving this award' to Neil and Neil announces that he is happy to receive this award from Sonia. Sheena is not pleased with this. She asks Neil as soon as possible as he comes to his seat. 'Do you know this Sonia Neil, Yes, Ive met her before replies Neil. Sheena inyerested to know more asks him 'Where and How?' I was invited to her assignment success party remember that party where l was invited as a chief guest, it was their party, Sheena says 'Oh I see and adds further 'She is a pretty lady .Neil replies 'Yes she's very pretty ' and sheena looks at him as Neil looks towards Sonia . Pictures of Neil and Sonia are published in the newspapers .The next day of the award function .Mr Tandon talks of the picture in the paper while Neil takes a look at them as Sheena walks in. Sheena a bit jealous says 'I don't know why the media is giving importance to this importance to this upcoming model along with commenting about you . Neil tells her 'Oh come on Sheena you're being rude, everyone deserves their share of limelight . To which Sheena replies 'So we have a Sonia's fan over here. ' Neil says 'Sheena , come on.' Sheena says 'Alright come on, let's go. Sonia's father sees the pictures in the newspaper and asks Sonia if she has met Neil before. She says that she met him at their success party. He tells her that their production company company was considering Neil for their film . Sonia says 'Oh , I see .' Do you want to come to my office Sonia. Sonia says 'No daddy I'mmeeting Ron for lunch today as he's leaving tomorrow ' Okay Sonia says her father. So I'll meet you later. Sonia says 'Bye Daddy. ' Sonia meets Ron for lunch .She tells him 'So Ron you have another assignment lined. I hope you enjoy your new work . Yes Sonia Ron says and adds further 'I hope so too. I wish you would also be there with me. ' Sonia tells him 'Well its not like , I'll be away.' I should leave in some time too.' Ron tells her 'Well

Sonia thanks for spending the afternoon with me. ' She tells him 'Ron , why don't you join daddy and me for dinner tonight. 'Ron joins Sonia and her father for dinner. Ron tells her father that they've been dating. Sonia's father tells him 'I knew you'll were close. ' But we haven't moved further. 'Ron added as Sonia needs time. 'Ron arrives to pickup Sonia 'Hello Sir Ron greets Sonia's father. Mr Roy greets him and asks him if he intends to be there longer to which Ron says 'Oh no Sir, I'll be going back the day after I was just waiting for this function . Sonia and Ron then leave for the function while Ron and Sonia arrive at the function. Neil and Sonia are getting ready to attend the award function . Neil has come over to pickup Sheena. Hello Sheena Neil tells her 'Are you ready to leave?' 'Yes Neil Sheena replies 'How was your shoot?' Sheena asks him about his shoot of their movie together. She further says 'You still have few more days of your shoot, before i join the shoot. Neil says 'Yes sometime more. 'Sheena says in that way I'll be able to spend some more time with you .'Yes Sheena replies Neil.Neil and Sheena arrive at the function. Sheena tells Neil 'The last time I went out with you to Reena's party you didn't like the outfit, I hope you like this one Neil. Neil says 'Well Sheena .'I'm sorry about that day says Sheena. It's okay Neil tells her it's in the past . Sheena says further 'No really I just thought of it now Neil smilesand says' Alright Sheena'. Neil spots Ron and Sonia at the awards function and Sonia notices Neil as well . Sonia smiles at Neil. Sonia keeps looking towards Neil which even Neil. Sonia and Ron are joined by certain common friends. The function begins and Neil happens to get happens to get an award for which Sonia is called on stage. Sonia who was happy with her recognition that she was getting from her assignment says 'Congratulations on receiving this award' to Neil and Neil announces that he is happy to receive this award from Sonia. Sheena is not pleased with this. She asks Neil as soon as possible as he comes to his seat. 'Do you know this Sonia Neil, Yes, Ive met her before replies Neil. Sheena inyerested to know more asks him 'Where and How?' I was invited to her assignment success party remember that party where l was invited as a chief guest, it was their party, Sheena says 'Oh I see and adds further 'She is a pretty lady .Neil replies 'Yes she's very pretty ' and sheena looks at him as Neil looks towards Sonia . Pictures of Neil and Sonia are published in the newspapers .The next day of the award function .Mr Tandon talks of the picture in the paper while Neil takes a look at them as Sheena walks in. Sheena a bit jealous says 'I don't know why the media is giving importance to this importance to this upcoming model along with commenting about you . Neil tells her 'Oh come on Sheena you're being rude, everyone deserves their share of limelight . To which Sheena replies 'So we have a Sonia's fan over here. ' Neil says 'Sheena , come on.' Sheena says 'Alright come on, let's go. Sonia's father sees the pictures in the newspaper and asks Sonia if she has met Neil before. She says that she met him at their success party. He tells her that their production company company was considering Neil for their film . Sonia says 'Oh , I see .' Do you want to come to my office Sonia. Sonia says 'No daddy I'mmeeting Ron for lunch today as he's leaving tomorrow ' Okay Sonia says her father. So I'll meet you later. Sonia says 'Bye Daddy. ' Sonia meets Ron for lunch .She tells him 'So Ron you have another assignment lined. I hope you enjoy your new work . Yes Sonia Ron says and adds further 'I hope so too. I wish you would also be there with me. ' Sonia tells him 'Well its not like , I'll be away.' I should leave in some time too.' Ron tells her 'Well Sonia thanks for spending the afternoon with me. ' She tells him 'Ron , why don't you join daddy and me for dinner tonight. 'Ron joins Sonia and her father for dinner. Ron tells her father that they've been dating. Sonia's father tells him 'I knew you'll were close. ' But we haven't moved further. 'Ron added as Sonia needs time. '

Space of Chapter 4

Space area

Chapter 5

Sonia's father says I see and asks him 'So are you getting back to work ?' Ron says 'Yes Sir' . Sonia tells him that she will drop him to the airport. Ron says 'Alright Sonia.' At Sonia's father father's production company they go through the photos of Neil and Sonia and tell him that Neil and Sonia should be cast in their film together as they were very impressed with the media reports. Sonia's father tells them that Sonia is not interested in taking this film, however they can go ahead with Neil. They say 'Mr Roy please ask Sonia to consider her decision again, we think Sonia should work with Neil in your first film.' Mr Roy says 'Alright I 'll tell her this.'.

Mr Roy tells. Sonia, she should definitely rethink her decision to act in his film as they all wanted her to act with Neil as they liked her photos with him and they've decided to take Neil for the film. Sonia thinks and says 'But daddy'...suddenly her father says'Don't think much Sonia, I wouldn't like it any other way thanmy daughter acting in my film. Sonia pausing'Eh , okay... daddy' .Her father tells her I'm so happy with your decision Sonia's father breaks the news to his production house that Sonia has made up her mind to do his film. The production people arevery happy with her decision and tell him that they should go ahead with approaching Neil for the role Sonia's father agrees with them. Sonia's father arranges a meeting with Neil.Mr Tandon tells Neil that there is an offer from Sonia's father's production company. He says to fix.a time to meet them.How about eleven am the day after. That's ok, whatabout the shoot that day?' It's onlyat 2 pm saysMr Tandon. Neilsays 'That's fine then Mr Tandon.' Mr Tandon accompanies Neil to Sonia's father's production company . They discuss the project with the production people and Neil is satisfied with the project. Sonia's father says that he would like to start the project as soon as possible as it is his first project. Neil says that Mr Tandon would let them know, and tells Mr Tandon 'Mr Tandon please inform them about the schedule.' Sonia's father says 'My daughter is the actress that will work in this movie. Neil says 'That's not of importance to me. I generally don't look into these matters. But I'm sure she'll do a good job.'

Sonia's father is happy to know what Neil had to say about Sonia. He tells him 'Thankyou Neil I'm taking this as a compliment . Neil says 'Yes definitely, I've seen her current project .'

Space of Chapter 5

Space area

Chapter 6

Sonia officially becomes part of her father's project. She tells the production people that she is ready to start anytime. Meanwhile Mr Tandon tells Neil that he has informed Sonia's father's production house that Neil would start working on this project immediately. He says 'Sure Mr Tandon , Sheena is not pleased that Neil is going to begin work with Sonia in between his other projects . 'Neil are you sure you want to do this project? She asks .They are even working for the first time. She adds further. Neil says 'Sheena I like the project you know such matters don't matter to me .'

Sheena upset says that I hope you know what you're doing Neil.' Sonia tells her father that she's looking forward to working with his project now that she has decided . She even tells Ron that she is about to work in her father's project. Ron is surprised and he tells her 'I didn't expect this .'I thought you weren't interested in this project. Sonia tells him "I thought so, but everyone here felt I should work with Neil so I took it up for my daddy .'.Ron not so comfortable listening to this hangs the phone saying 'Oh , eh pauses and asks her 'So will you be coming here?' Sonia says 'No Ron ; I'm beginning work immediately, I may come after my first schedule.' Ron , not so pleased says 'Bye Sonia I'll speak to you later.'

Space of Chapter 6

Space area

Chapter 7

Sonia is eager to begin work on the first day of the project as she wanted to do her best for her father's first production work. Her father tells her so are you ready to leave ?I'm glad you're not nervous.' Sonia says 'No,daddy I'm not . Let's go Sonia.' Sonia and her father reach the shooting spot. Neil arrives as well. As they get ready for the shoot . Neil comes to Sonia and says 'Hello ' Sonia, how are you feeling considering this is your first film with your father that too.?' Sonia says that she is looking forward to begin and Neil tells her 'That's good Sonia'.

Their shoot begins and Sonia is happy that the shoot went well. At the end of the shoot for the day, she feels the attraction that she felt towards Neil before and feels like she wants to spend more time with him.Neil comes to her before leaving 'Bye Sonia ' he says. Sonia pausing says 'Eh ..Bye Neil'.

Neil notices the look on Sonia's face and asks her 'What happened Sonia?' Sonia says pausing again 'Eh nothing and tells him ' Good day Neil, I should also be going now.'

Space of Chapter 7

Space area

End of Part 1

To know more about the lives of Neil, Sonia, Ron and Sheena, stay connected with me,

Kavita Thomas

End

Official End